Made by RAFFI

Craig Pomranz
Illustrated by Margaret Chamberlain

F

FRANCES LINCOLN
CHILDREN'S BOOKS

Raffi lived with his mum and
his dad and his dog Scamp.
He liked giving Mum and Dad
GREAT BIG HUGS – and he could
run nearly as fast as Scamp.

But Raffi also asked a lot of questions....

SHERIE

BARRY

EDIE

MEL

RUBY

Who am I ?

SYLVIE

WHY did he feel different from the other children at school? Was it because he was the smallest in his class? Or because his hair was longer than the other boys'? Could it be because he liked wearing bright colours?

'Maybe everyone feels different,' Raffi thought to himself.

MEG

GERRY

The other kids were always tumbling
about, throwing things and yelling at
each other. But Raffi didn't like noise
and rough play.

So at playtime Raffi often liked to sit
by himself, or find a teacher to stand with,
just for a little peace and quiet.

One day it was even noisier than usual in the playground. Raffi looked for a quiet spot and saw Miss Fernandez.

"What are you doing?" he asked.
"I'm knitting a scarf for my sister," she replied, smiling.
"That's beautiful," said Raffi. "Is it hard to do?"
"It just takes practice and patience,"
said Miss Fernandez. "Do you want me
to show you?"
"YES, PLEASE!" said Raffi.

So Miss Fernandez
put the needles
into Raffi's hands.

First the wool tickled,
then he got it all tangled.

Raffi was upset!

But Miss Fernandez said, "Don't worry, Raffi.
You didn't hurt the scarf. To fix it, you just unknit
the stitches and start again. It's called *tinking* –
that's *knit* backwards!"

They both laughed,
and she helped Raffi
untangle the wool.
Then he tried again –
and this time it worked.
He was knitting!
And he loved it.

Raffi couldn't wait to tell Mum
and Dad about knitting.
He ran home from the bus stop
and burst into the kitchen.

"Miss Fernandez showed me how to knit and it was really easy," he told them. "Can we get some needles and wool?

PLEASE?"

At the wool shop there were so many
beautiful colours of wool.
When Raffi looked for red,
he found Crimson, Magenta and lots
of other colours. And it was the same
with the shades of blue and green.
There was Jade and Emerald
and Turquoise and Aqua...

Raffi loved all the colours and the names.
Then he had a great idea. He grabbed
one of each colour. It would be so cool
to make a scarf for Dad's birthday,
with all the colours of the rainbow.

Soon Raffi was knitting everywhere – in his bed,
in the bathroom, at breakfast...
even on the school bus.

It was a long way to school and some of the
children teased him. And it didn't help that
Dad's scarf grew to four metres long and trailed
all down the aisle of the bus. Ruby almost
tripped over it, and all the children laughed.

But Raffi just wrapped the scarf round
his neck three times and kept on knitting.

That night at bedtime, Raffi had some more questions for Mum...

And Raffi snuggled down in his bed and went to sleep.

Next day at school, something happened that changed everything. Mrs O'Donnell said the class was going to put on a play. Barry would be a prince and Ruby would be a princess.

Raffi put up his hand.
"Miss?" he called out. "If Barry is a prince,
won't he need a royal cape?"
"That would be nice, Raffi," said Mrs O'Donnell,
"but we don't have a lot of time. Let's learn
our lines and see if we can perform the play
on Friday. That's only four days away."

After school Raffi couldn't wait to get home. He asked Mum if she would help him find some old sheets or tablecloths.

They found some yellow cotton fabric and a beautiful piece of purple velvet. Raffi took it all up to his room – and this is what he did....

He took a chair and draped the fabric over it.

Then he took some pins and pinned the fabric together.

It was purple on one side, and yellow on the other side – and it made an elegant velvet cape with a beautiful yellow lining. Now Raffi just had to sew it together.

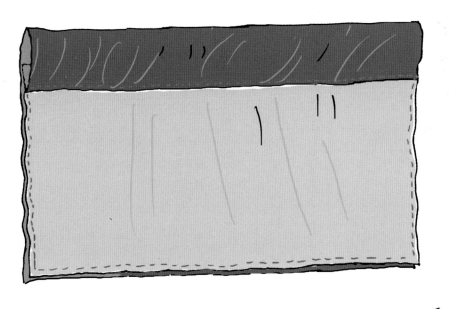

He sewed round the cape as best he could. Then he folded the velvet over twice at the top to make a collar.

Finally Raffi sewed the collar to the cape and threaded a ribbon through the hole in the collar, with a safety pin.

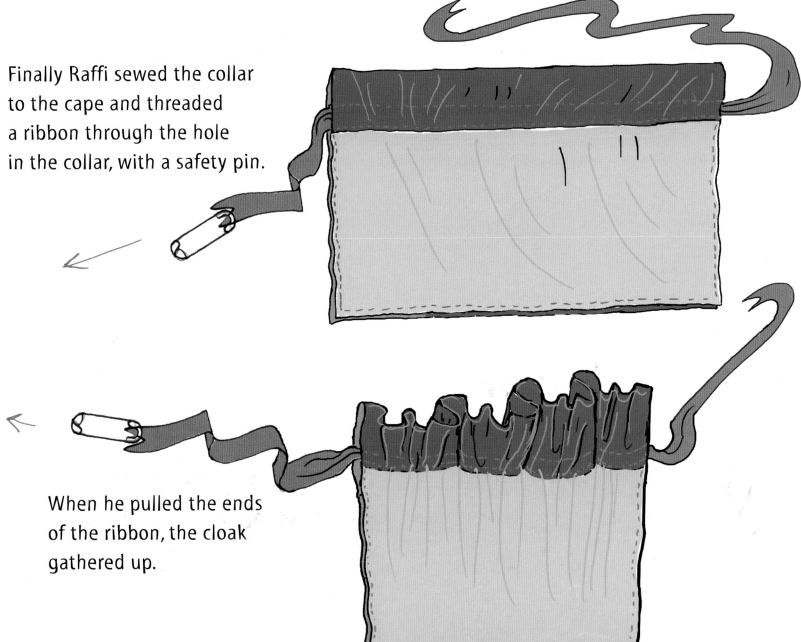

When he pulled the ends of the ribbon, the cloak gathered up.

Later that evening, Mum and Dad got a big surprise.
There was Raffi, peeping round the door with
a huge grin on his face.
"Madam! Sir!" announced Raffi. "Ta dah!
This is a royal cape – for the prince to wear
in the school play."

Raffi's mum and dad looked
at the cape in amazement.
The collar stood tall and the cape
swished and...

it truly was a cape fit for a prince!

Next morning Raffi stuffed the cape in his
knitting bag and ran to the bus.
"What you got there?" Gerry asked, sniggering.
"Hey, Raf, your bag got fat!" Ruby shouted.
"It's almost as big as Gerry," snorted Barry.
That almost started a fight.

But Raffi just held tight to his bag.

At school he ran to Mrs O'Donnell.
"Please, Miss, I have something for you."
Mrs O'Donnell opened the bag slowly.
"A cape!" she exclaimed. "Did you really
make this? Raffi, it's amazing."

All of a sudden everyone wanted to look.

"Wait a minute!" said Barry, pushing in.
"I'm the prince!" And he grabbed the cape
and put it on.

Then Raffi explained to everyone how
he had found fabric at home and sewed it
all by himself.

Raffi listened happily to all the chatter.
'Hmmm,' he thought, 'maybe I could
be a famous designer one day!'

On Dad's birthday, Raffi gave him
the long rainbow-coloured scarf.
Dad loved it!

And on Raffi's birthday, Mum made labels for Raffi to use on his finished knitting and sewing projects...

Made by Raffi.

A few weeks later, while Raffi was sitting
in the playground, knitting as usual,
Barry's ball came rolling past.
Raffi picked it up and tossed it
back to him.